For Motoko

One evening about two hundred years ago, Johann Wolfgang von Goethe stopped at a tavern to dine. As he sat at his table, he gazed at the waitress who stood taking an order at a nearby table. Her red dress stood out in sharp contrast against the white wall behind her. When the waitress moved away, Goethe continued to stare in the same direction, at the wall.

Then a strange thing happened: on the white wall he saw a faint glowing image of the waitress's dress – but it was green, not red! Why? This moment of wonder led Goethe into more than twenty years of scientific research on color.

In 1810 he published *Farbenlehre*, his color theory. He determined that there were three primary colors – red, blue and yellow – from which all the other colors could be made, and that each color had an opposite, or complementary, color.

Goethe (1749 - 1832) is celebrated as a great German poet, novelist, and philosopher. But, to him, his color theory was his most important achievement.

ISBN 0-590-63587-5

Copyright © 1998 by Eric Carle. All rights reserved.
Published by Scholastic Inc., 555 Broadway, New York, NY 10012, by arrangement with Simon & Schuster Books for Young Readers, Simon & Schuster Children's Publishing Division.
SCHOLASTIC and associated logos are trademarks and/or registered trademarks of Scholastic Inc.

12 11 10 9 8 7 6 5 4 3 2 1   8 9/9 0 1 2 3/0

Printed in the U.S.A.

First Scholastic printing, October 1998

Eric Carle's name and signature logotype are trademarks of Eric Carle.
The text of this book is set in 15-point Lucida Sans Roman.
The illustrations are rendered in cut paper collage.

Ann Beneduce, consulting editor.

Hello, Red Fox

ERIC CARLE

SCHOLASTIC INC.
New York Toronto London Auckland Sydney

Important
In order to enjoy this book, follow these simple steps:
The pages should be fairly well-lighted.
Stare at the dot inside the red heart.
Slowly count to ten without moving your eyes.
Then move your eyes to the dot on the opposite blank page. Count to three.

•

A faint green heart will appear around the dot.
If you didn't see it, try again. Do it quietly and peacefully.
Close and rest your eyes for a moment before turning the page.
Now you are ready to enjoy the story.

"Your birthday is coming up," said Mama Frog.
"Let's have a party. A birthday party. Whom would you like to invite?"

Little Frog answered,
"I would like to invite my friends,
Red Fox, Purple Butterfly, Orange Cat,
Green Snake, Yellow Bird, Blue Fish,
and White Dog with Black Spots."

On Little Frog's birthday, his friends began to arrive.
"Hello, Red Fox," said Little Frog. "Welcome to my birthday party."
"Thank you for inviting me," said Red Fox.

"But this is not a red fox," said Mama Frog. "This is a green fox."
"Oh, Mama, you have not looked at the fox long enough," said Little Frog.
Mama Frog looked and looked at the fox for a long time...

...and, indeed, Little Frog was right!

"Hello, Purple Butterfly," said Little Frog. "Welcome to my birthday party."
"Thank you for inviting me," said Purple Butterfly.

"But this is not a purple butterfly," said Mama Frog. "This is a yellow butterfly."
"Oh, Mama, you have not looked at the butterfly long enough," said Little Frog.
Mama Frog looked and looked at the butterfly for a long time...

...and, indeed, Little Frog was right!

"Hello, Orange Cat," said Little Frog. "Welcome to my birthday party."
"Thank you for inviting me," said Orange Cat.

"But this is not an orange cat," said Mama Frog. "This is a blue cat."
"Oh, Mama, you have not looked at the cat long enough," said Little Frog.
Mama Frog looked and looked at the cat for a long time...

...and, indeed, Little Frog was right!

"Hello, Green Snake," said Little Frog. "Welcome to my birthday party."
"Thank you for inviting me," said Green Snake.

"But this is not a green snake," said Mama Frog. "This is a red snake."
"Oh, Mama, you have not looked at the snake long enough," said Little Frog.
Mama Frog looked and looked at the snake for a long time...

...and, indeed, Little Frog was right!

"Hello, Yellow Bird," said Little Frog. "Welcome to my birthday party."
"Thank you for inviting me," said Yellow Bird.

"But this is not a yellow bird," said Mama Frog. "This is a purple bird."
"Oh, Mama, you have not looked at the bird long enough," said Little Frog.
Mama Frog looked and looked at the bird for a long time...

...and, indeed, Little Frog was right!

"Hello, Blue Fish," said Little Frog. "Welcome to my birthday party."
"Thank you for inviting me," said Blue Fish.

"But this is not a blue fish," said Mama Frog. "This is an orange fish."
"Oh, Mama, you have not looked at the fish long enough," said Little Frog.
Mama Frog looked and looked at the fish for a long time ...

...and, indeed, Little Frog was right!

"Hello, White Dog with Black Spots," said Little Frog. "Welcome to my birthday party."
"Thank you for inviting me," said White Dog with Black Spots.

"But this is not a white dog with black spots," said Mama Frog.
"This is a black dog with white spots."
"Oh, Mama, you have not looked at the dog long enough," said Little Frog.
Mama Frog looked and looked at the dog for a long time...

...and, indeed, Little Frog was right!

"And for the birthday child," said Mama Frog, "a red flower with green leaves."

"But this is not a red flower with green leaves," said Little Frog.
"Oh, Little Frog, you have not looked at the flower long enough," said Mama Frog.
Little Frog looked and looked at the flower for a long time...

...and, indeed, Mama Frog was right!

Then Mama Frog kissed Little Frog in front of all his friends.

And Little Frog blushed.

Happy Birthday, Little Frog!

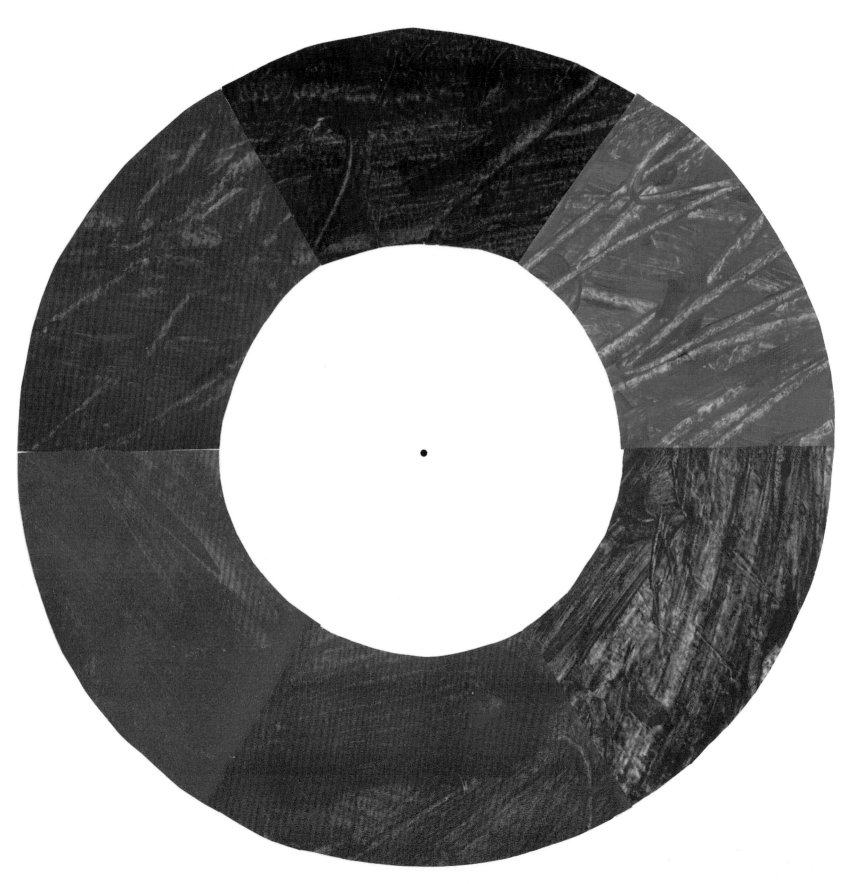

Based on Goethe's Color Wheel